The Moon in my Tea Cup

SHWETA KALI JYOTI

Be You Bee

The Little Ones Enchanted Collection — Leaf One

Custard Fairy Group, Inc.

Los Angeles, California

Published by Shweta Kali Jyoti / Custard Fairy Group, Inc.
Los Angeles, California
www.custardfairy.com

Publisher's Note: This is a work of fiction. Names, characters, places, and incidents are the product of the author's imagination. Locales and public names are sometimes used for atmospheric purposes. Any resemblance to actual persons, living or dead, or to businesses, companies, events, institutions, or locales is entirely coincidental.

Book design by Mayur Heganekar.

The Moon in My Teacup / Shweta Kali Jyoti — 1st ed.
The Little Ones Enchanted Collection — Leaf One
ISBN: 978-0-9978370-1-8

----

*The Little Ones Enchanted Collection is the voice of runes—
echoes of memory, laughter, and happiness—
woven into tales where childhood shines with wonder. *

Printed in the United States of America.

Dedicated to my soul sister

One night, I saw the moon.
But she wasn't in the sky.
She was in the lake.

"Moon!" I called. "Come out of the water! I want to visit you in the sky."

But the moon shimmered and said,
"If I want to float in the lake,
then let me float in the lake.
I like it here."

I blinked and looked up.
There she was—
in the sky and in the water,
twinkling in both places at once.

"How are you doing that?" I asked.
"You're in the sky and the lake at the same time!"

Jump into the
lake... or leap
into sky!

The moon giggled,
"If you want to be with me,
then jump into the lake...
or leap into the sky!"

I scratched my head.
"I don't think people can just... jump into the sky.
Or lakes. I'd get all wet!"

8

"Oh, dear," said the moon.
"You're thinking again.
Too much thinking!
Stop. Stop. Stop!"

I crossed my arms.
"Are you seriously telling me to stop thinking?"

She nodded.
"Stop trying to catch me with your brain.
Try with your heart."

What a strange moon.
I looked in the lake—there she was.
I looked in the sky—there she was again!

"Okay," I said. "I'll try."
I crouched. I jumped!

But the moon slipped through
my fingers like water.
She laughed. "Try again!"

So I made a cup of blue tea.
I took it outside and sat very still.

The surface of the tea was smooth—
like a tiny lake in a cup.

And there—
just like in the real lake—
was the moon.

Floating, shimmering,
right there in my teacup!

"Moon," I said,
"You're everywhere, aren't you?
First the lake, then the sky...
now my tea?"

The moon didn't answer.
But I am sure I saw her wink.

So I did something silly.
I drank the tea.

Sip by sip...
the moon slipped inside me.

And just like that,
she melted into moon-rays,
spinning soft and quiet
within my heart.

I laughed.

The moon laughed too.
"Tricked you!" I said.

"No," said the moon,
"I tricked you!"

And then we both laughed,
because maybe...
just maybe...
we tricked each other.

24

Or maybe—
the truth is
the moon lives in everything.
The sky,
the lake,
a teacup...
and even you and me.

Discover More in
The Little Ones Enchanted Collection.

A series of lyrical, dreamlike tales that celebrate childhood wonder and the quiet magic of everyday life.

Available titles:

The Moon in My Teacup

The Star in My Pocket

The Wind in My Shoes

The Rainbow on My Window

The Sky Tea Ceremony

Each story is crafted to be read aloud and cherished, inviting children and families into worlds of gentle enchantment.

Be You Bee